ADVENTURES
IN THE
KINGDOM™

IN SEARCH
OF
WANDERER

Written by Dian Layton.
Illustrations created by Al Berg.

Illustrations created by Al Berg.

Published by MercyPlace Ministries

MercyPlace is a licensed imprint of Destiny Image® Inc.

Distributed by

Destiny Image® Publishers, Inc.
P.O. Box 310
Shippensburg, PA 17257-0310

ISBN 0-9677402-8-2

For Worldwide Distribution
Printed in the U.S.A.

This book and all other Destiny Image, Revival Press, MercyPlace, Fresh Bread, Destiny Image Fiction, and Treasure House books are available at Christian bookstores and distributors worldwide.

For a U.S. bookstore nearest you, call **1-800-722-6774**.
For more information on foreign distributors, call **717-532-3040**.
Or reach us on the Internet: **www.seeker.org**

CONTENTS

Gladness

Glee

Giggles

Do

Doodle

Yes

Dawdle

Seeker

Slow

HopeSo

KnowSo

vi

The King

Daring

Moira

CHAPTER ONE

Seeker looked again at the photograph of his family. Why couldn't things have stayed the way they were in that picture? Why did his dad have to go away?

Seeker's father's name was Wanderer. Wanderer used to live in the Kingdom...he used to live at home...but not anymore. Seeker wasn't sure what had happened; he just knew that he REALLY missed his dad. With a deep sigh, Seeker tucked the picture back into his shirt pocket and kept walking toward Royal Harbor.

Just then, two familiar voices called, "Hey, Seeker! Wait for us!" Seeker turned to see his friends, Doodle and Do, running toward him. Seeker waved and smiled as the two brothers tried to out-"DO" each other at running. Doodle reached him first, excitedly holding up two lanterns. "Look what I have, Seeker!"

Do came panting up from behind, also holding two lanterns. "Me, too! Look at my lanterns! Daring told us to bring these in case we need extra ones for the club meeting today!"

Seeker was impressed. "Lanterns? I wonder where Daring is planning to take us this time?"

Doodle and Do's brother, Daring, was a royal officer in the King's service on the sea. Daring used to be gone for months at a time, but now he lived in Royal Harbor and only went sailing when the King sent him out on special adventures.

"DO you remember that time when we REALLY needed fifteen coins so we could go and see Daring?" Doodle asked.

"I sure DO!" his brother responded.

"I'll *never* forget that!" Seeker said. "But now you can see your brother whenever you want! We all can! Let's get going, or we'll be late!"

The boys hurried toward Royal Harbor for the Adventure Club meeting. Once a week after school, Seeker and his friends had been getting together aboard the tall sailing ship *The Adventurer*. Daring had served so faithfully that the King had given him his very own ship.

Now in port at Royal Harbor, *The Adventurer* had become the favorite meeting place for the children.

When they reached Royal Harbor, Seeker slowed to a walk, but Doodle and Do raced toward the pier where their other friends were leaning against the railing. Giggles, Gladness and Glee were laughing, like usual. Dawdle and Slow were quietly tossing cracker crumbs to the sea gulls. HopeSo, KnowSo and Yes were trying to guess how big the ship was and how fast it could go.

Seeker breathed in deeply the saltwater air and smiled as he watched Doodle and Do showing their lanterns to the other children. Then Seeker looked past his friends to the familiar wooden ship tied to the dock. Gentle waves slapped the sides of *The Adventurer* and its three huge sails billowed in the wind, as if longing to leave the port. Daring was standing on the deck, waving. "Come aboard!" he shouted.

Everyone laughed and waved back as they hurried over the gangplank and onto the deck of the tall ship. "Wait for me!" The children turned to see Moira hurrying across the pier. (Seeker's sister, Moira, had been helping Daring every week with the Adventure Club.)

"Okay," Daring nodded. "Everyone is here! Do you remember the song we learned last week?"

"I should HOPE so!" said HopeSo.

"I KNOW so!" said KnowSo (in his most confident voice).

Their sister laughed, "YES! YES, of course we do! It's called 'The Attitude of Gratitude'!"

"And it's what we're going to DO!" called Doodle and Do as they led the others in singing:

Help me always trust the Ki-ng;

When life seems dark, or sad de-spair-ing!

In his light the darkness lea-ves

Instead of crying - I will choose to sing!

I will overcome the obstacles with opposites!

Overcome the obstacles with opposites!

Overcome the obstacles with opposites -

In my life all the time!

I want an attitude of gratitude!

I want an attitude of gratitude!

I want an attitude of gratitude In my heart all the time.

Doodle do do do, Doodle do do do; Doodle do do do,

Doodle do do do!

5

Doodle and Do did a little sailor jig during the last chorus. The other children laughed until their stomachs hurt; and the more they laughed, the more Doodle and Do added to their dance! The two brothers loved having an audience.

"Wonderful!" Moira said, applauding. "And now for the Adventure Club drill! Attention!"

The children lined up and saluted.

"Adventure Club members have an attitude of gratitude!" she called.

"Attitude of gratitude!" the children responded together.

6

"Adventure Club members overcome obstacles with opposites!" she announced.

The children nodded and saluted. "Overcome obstacles with opposites!"

"You overcome darkness with…?" Moira asked.

"Light!" the children shouted together.

"You overcome evil with…?"

"Good!"

"You overcome greed with…?"

"Giving!"

"You overcome sadness with…?"

"Gladness!"

As everyone laughed and patted Gladness on the back, Daring called, "It's time for today's adventure! Each of you will need to carry a lantern with you. Help yourselves to the ones sitting over there on the wooden crates; and Doodle and Do brought extra ones so we would have enough."

As the children each picked up a lantern they talked excitedly. "Where are we going today?" "It must be some place dark if we need lanterns."

Yes was nervous. "I hope it's not too dark—I get scared sometimes when it's dark!"

Moira put an arm around the younger girl's shoulder and smiled reassuringly. "Don't worry—we're all together!"

Daring picked up the picnic basket. "After the adventure we'll come back here and give you time to work on your model ships!"

Seeker was relieved. "Great! I've almost finished mine and I want to take it home today!" The children had all been working hard the past few weeks on building small wooden ships.

They followed Daring and Moira over the gangplank and back onto the shore. "Wh-wh-where are we going?" asked Dawdle.

Daring smiled at Dawdle. "Caves," he responded, in a low mysterious voice.

"Caves?!" the children echoed.

Daring nodded. "Caves."

CHAPTER TWO

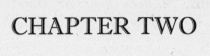

Between Royal Harbor and the Castle of Joy and Peace was an underground passageway with a maze of tunnels and caves. Daring had spent many childhood days exploring these. Today he led Moira and the children to a steep cliff at the edge of Royal Harbor, where an entrance to the passageway was hidden behind some trees and bushes. When they reached the entrance, the children were very happy to find someone waiting to meet them...

"King! Hi!" Giggles, Gladness and Glee reached him first, and laughed as the King picked each of them up and twirled them in the air. The others all crowded around for a group hug.

Then the King opened the door to the passageway and smiled one of his mysterious smiles. "Shall we?" he asked, and everyone followed the King through the entrance.

"S-S-Sure is d-d-dark in here!" called Slow as she and the others lit their lanterns.

Glee laughed and held her lantern high. "You overcome darkness with...?"

"Light!" the others responded.

Yes reached out to the King. "And you overcome fear of the dark by holding the King's hand!"

The King smiled. "Alright now everyone, there are hundreds of tunnels that lead off from the main passageway, so follow me and stay close together!" The King led the way through the rocky hall. Daring, Moira, and the children "oohed" and "ahhed" over the beautiful rock formations. Stalactites and stalagmites decorated the tunnel with a golden glow under the light of the lanterns.

After many long moments of walking, the King stooped to enter a low doorway. "Cave," KnowSo whispered knowingly. Yes nodded. She had been walking confidently far down the line, but now hurried once again to take hold of the King's hand.

The children were surprised and happy to find a low rocky shelf around the wall of the cave. It was a perfect place to sit down.

The King stood in the middle of the cave and everyone looked at him. "I want you to experience something for a few moments," he said. "Darkness."

"Darkness?" Yes echoed, holding more tightly to his hand.

"Darkness," the King repeated. He looked around at the children's faces and asked, "Do you trust me?"

"Yes, we DO!" everyone responded, with Doodle and Do's voices loudest of all.

"Then blow out your lanterns," said the King.

Everyone blew out their lanterns. Immediately, they were in total darkness. It was darker than any darkness they had ever been in before. Giggles, Gladness and Glee giggled nervously.

"This is how some people live their lives," the King said. "In complete darkness."

"That would be very scary," Yes's voice trembled slightly.

"You know my Kingdom as Joy and Peace," said the King. It is also the Kingdom of Light. Everyone who really knows me, lives in the Light. But the people who don't know me…"

"Live in darkness." KnowSo said, finishing the sentence.

"That would be a very sad place to live, "Moira said softly. "I never want to live in Darkness!"

"Stay close to me, Moira," said the King, "and you won't live in Darkness."

"Did the people of Greed live in the Darkness, King?" KnowSo asked, remembering how the children had destroyed the dragon Greed with giving and the people moved to Generosity.

"Yes," the King responded. "And many years ago, your families lived in the Darkness of Fear."

"My mom told me all about that," said Seeker. "The dragon Fear controlled everyone there!"

"Please don't talk anymore about dragons!" Yes said, clutching tightly to the King's hand.

"DO you think there are more dragons out there, King?" Doodle asked excitedly.

"Many more dragons, Doodle," the King answered. "They rule the Darkness and try to keep people blinded, so they cannot see my Light."

With that the King lit a lantern. The warm glow shone on His face as He spoke solemnly, "Too many people spend their lives in the Darkness, going through a maze of endless tunnels and caverns." Then the King looked directly at Moira and Seeker. "Some people spend their lives *wandering*, never finding their way to Joy and Peace in my Kingdom."

13

When the King said the word *wandering*, Seeker and Moira caught their breath. "Wandering," Seeker whispered. Moira reached out and gave her brother's hand a quick squeeze. Seeker touched the pocket where the picture of his family was safely tucked. "Wanderer," he said, looking at Moira.

Moira felt the familiar stab of pain in her heart. Although she had tried to be strong for Seeker's sake, the long months without her father had been difficult for Moira. Lately she had been telling herself to just accept the fact that he was gone and get on with her life. She had been trying to overcome the pain by not thinking about it; but it wasn't working very well.

Daring and the children explored the cave, and the King sat down beside Seeker and Moira. "Dad is living in Darkness, isn't he, King?" Seeker asked.

The King nodded and Moira said, "Dragons. Are there dragons keeping him in the Darkness, King?"

The King nodded again. "There are dragons, Moira," he said, "but they aren't *making* your father stay in Darkness He is *choosing* to stay there." The King looked deep into Moira's eyes and said, "Living in Darkness, or living in my Kingdom is a choice that each person must make."

"My heart hurts, King," Seeker said. "It *really* hurts."

14

The King very gently touched Seeker's heart. A deep warmth filled him and Seeker felt his pain get smaller. "Thanks, King," he whispered.

Then the King reached out to touch Moira's heart but she stopped him, took hold of both his hands, and said, "It's okay, King. I'm fine."

A look of concern flashed through the King's eyes. "You must come and talk to me about how you *really* feel, Moira," he said.

Moira nodded and quickly wiped away the tears that had suddenly spilled out of her eyes. "Okay, King, I'll do that...sometime soon... I promise. I'll come and talk to you."

By now, some of the other children had been watching quietly. "DO you think Wanderer will ever come home?" Do whispered.

"I HOPE so!" said HopeSo.

"I KNOW so!" said KnowSo confidently.

"Yes, yes of course he will!" Yes nodded, going to sit close to Moira. Glee followed her and the two young girls looked sadly at Moira. They loved Seeker's sister and wished they could help.

After exploring a few more tunnels and caves, the King led them out through the passageways, and back toward Royal Harbor. When they reached the entrance, the King waved good-bye and the children continued on to *The Adventurer*. The children were anxious to work on their model ships.

CHAPTER THREE

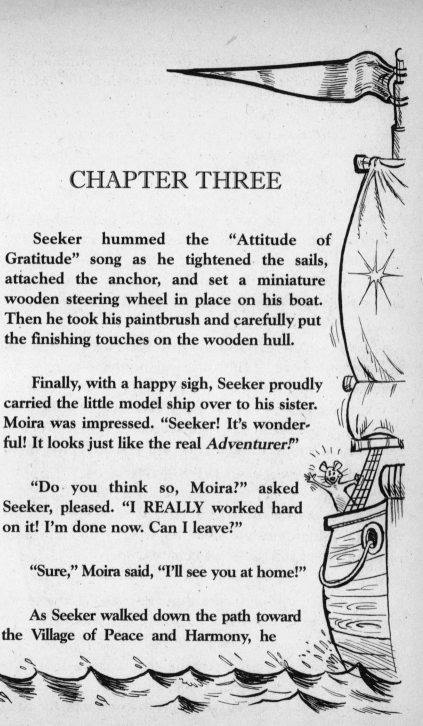

Seeker hummed the "Attitude of Gratitude" song as he tightened the sails, attached the anchor, and set a miniature wooden steering wheel in place on his boat. Then he took his paintbrush and carefully put the finishing touches on the wooden hull.

Finally, with a happy sigh, Seeker proudly carried the little model ship over to his sister. Moira was impressed. "Seeker! It's wonderful! It looks just like the real *Adventurer!*"

"Do you think so, Moira?" asked Seeker, pleased. "I REALLY worked hard on it! I'm done now. Can I leave?"

"Sure," Moira said, "I'll see you at home!"

As Seeker walked down the path toward the Village of Peace and Harmony, he

17

thought about the "Attitude of Gratitude" song. He had sung the words so many times, but had never really thought about what they meant, until now. "Hmm…" Seeker said aloud, "An attitude of gratitude in my heart all the time. I wonder how you can have an attitude of gratitude in your heart *all* the time? How are you supposed to be thankful *all* the time? Especially…especially…"

Seeker sat down on a rock near the path and set his model ship beside him. He reached inside his shirt pocket and pulled out the little picture of his family. On one side of the photograph were Moira and his mother, Contentment; on the other side were Seeker and his father…Wanderer.

Seeker shook his head and held back tears that began to form in his eyes. "How are you supposed to have an attitude of gratitude about something like this?! How are you supposed to be happy when you haven't seen your dad for a long, long time? He never writes; he doesn't even send you a birthday card! How are you supposed to be glad that your dad's name is Wanderer?!"

Seeker angrily stuffed the picture back into his shirt pocket. "I don't feel like going home yet," he said aloud. "I think I'll go and see if my boat will float."

He picked up the model ship and went to one of his favorite places. It was the stream behind the castle.

Seeker had a special spot at the stream where he and the King often went fishing and skipping rocks. The first day when Seeker had begun to really get to know him, the King

18

had brought him here. The King had explained how water from the Throne Room fountain tumbled down an underground waterfall and flowed out into the stream, where everyone in the Kingdom could enjoy the clear fresh water.

At this particular place, the stream was quite shallow. Seeker pulled his shoes off and rolled up his pant legs, and then, very carefully, set the small wooden boat onto the water. Sure enough—it floated! Up and down it bobbed along, like a real ship out on the open sea. Seeker sat down on the grassy shore beside the stream and watched. "Hmm...I sure wish Dad could see my boat! He always liked making things, too. We sure had some good times together."

Seeker lay down on the grass and rolled over onto his back. White puffy clouds moved slowly across the sky above him. Seeker liked to watch clouds, and think about what each fluffy shape reminded him of. Today many of the clouds were in the shapes of animals. Seeker thought about the wooden carvings on his bedroom shelf that his dad had made for him. There were dozens of little animals and all sizes of castles and miniature wooden soldiers; but Seeker's favorite carving was one of himself and his dad running together across a hill. Seeker's eyes filled with tears and he shut them tightly. "Dad," he whispered. "Dad, I miss you so much! Will you *ever* come home? Will I *ever* get to see you again?"

Seeker opened his eyes and blinked away the tears so that he could see. The clouds still moved slowly overhead. He looked at one especially big fluffy cloud. It looked like a ship...

A ship!

Oh, no! Seeker had been thinking so much about his father that he had forgotten to watch his model ship! He jumped to his feet and ran along the shore, desperately looking at the water. A short way downstream he saw the little boat. There it was—smashed against some rocks. Seeker hurried into the water and picked up the broken pieces.

"My boat! My boat! I worked so hard; and now it's wrecked!" The tears he had been holding back wouldn't stay inside any longer. "My boat! My boat!" he cried.

Then Seeker heard someone whistling. Oh, no! He didn't want anyone to know he had been crying, and he didn't want to have to explain why. Using his shirt-sleeve to wipe his nose, Seeker blinked hard and got ready to face whoever was coming. The whistling grew louder. Seeker took a deep breath and looked down the shore.

It was the King.

There he stood on the banks of the stream, looking at Seeker. The King smiled. It was a very, very gentle smile, and he kept whistling. The song he was whistling was "Attitude of Gratitude." All of a sudden Seeker felt angry. He ran toward the King, threw the broken boat on the ground and cried, "Don't you sing that song! It's an awful song! An awful song!"

The King reached out his great arms toward Seeker, but Seeker was filled with such hurt and anger that he pushed the King's arms away and pounded on the King's chest with his fists. The King stood very quietly and just let him do that. Then the tears came again, this time in such a flood that Seeker didn't even try to hold them back.

With a deep sob, Seeker's fists fell to his sides, and the King very gently took the boy in his arms, held him close, and just let him cry. The King put his hand on Seeker's heart. He had touched Seeker's heart earlier when they were in the cave, but now he seemed to touch pain that was even deeper inside. The King didn't ask Seeker to stop crying; he just held him and waited until Seeker had cried enough tears to wash some of the sadness and anger away.

Finally, Seeker blew his nose on a tissue that the King handed to him and said, "King, I don't understand. How am I supposed to have an attitude of gratitude? How am I supposed to be thankful? Look at my boat!" Seeker picked the pieces up from the ground. "I worked so hard; and now look at it—it's broken! How am I supposed to be thankful about *that*?"

"You can be thankful, Seeker, because I know how to *fix* boats."

Seeker was surprised. "You do?!"

The King nodded. "Yes. In fact, if you give me all the pieces and *really* trust me, I can fix *anything* that's broken."

"You can?" Seeker whispered, "Okay, King."

Seeker lifted up all the broken pieces of his boat and the King put them carefully into the pocket of his cloak. Then the King put out his big hand, and Seeker put his little hand into the King's big hand, and they walked toward the village. The "Attitude of Gratitude" song began to stir in Seeker's heart, slowly at first, but then stronger and stronger. He whistled with the King all the way to Peace and Harmony.

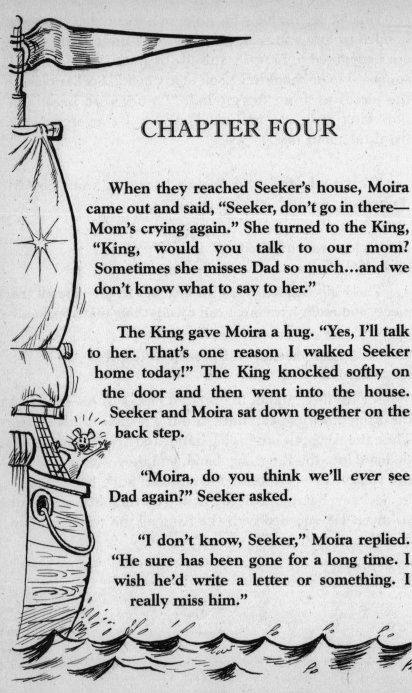

CHAPTER FOUR

When they reached Seeker's house, Moira came out and said, "Seeker, don't go in there—Mom's crying again." She turned to the King, "King, would you talk to our mom? Sometimes she misses Dad so much...and we don't know what to say to her."

The King gave Moira a hug. "Yes, I'll talk to her. That's one reason I walked Seeker home today!" The King knocked softly on the door and then went into the house. Seeker and Moira sat down together on the back step.

"Moira, do you think we'll *ever* see Dad again?" Seeker asked.

"I don't know, Seeker," Moira replied. "He sure has been gone for a long time. I wish he'd write a letter or something. I really miss him."

24

"Yeah, me too." Seeker sighed.

Moira looked at her brother for a moment and then spoke carefully. "Seeker...I think it's time for you to accept the facts. We might never see Dad again. Seeker, you have to realize that our family is broken."

Seeker sat straight up and looked at his sister with amazement. "What did you say?!"

"I said our family's broken, Seeker." Moira repeated sadly.

"Hooray!" Seeker cheered and jumped to his feet.

Moira stood beside him, confused. "Hooray? What do you mean 'hooray'?"

"I was just talking to the King! He said he could fix *anything* that's broken! It's a long story, but the King came and found me at the stream—my boat was broken...."

"Your boat was broken?" Moira repeated, shocked. "You mean your model ship? What happened?"

"Never mind right now!" Seeker said quickly, "The important thing is that the King said that he could fix *anything* that's broken! That means he could fix our family!"

Moira shook her head. "Oh, now, just a minute," she said, "I know that the King is *really* powerful—but fix our family? I don't know, Seeker. That's pretty hard, even for the King."

"No, it's not too hard! If he can fix anything that's broken, then he can fix our family! I know it! Listen, Moira, we've never REALLY asked him! It's like we've just given up on Dad; we haven't REALLY talked to the King about him!"

Moira was thoughtful. "You're right," she said. "We've never REALLY asked…"

"I have an idea!" Seeker said, "We could go to the Secret Place—you and I together—to the Secret Place every day and REALLY ask the King to bring Dad home!"

Moira smiled her agreement. "Okay, Seeker! It's certainly worth a try!"

The Secret Place is a special place where people can go and talk to the King. They don't always see him, but he is *always* there. Seeker had his very own Secret Place in one of the castle towers, and he and Moira began meeting there every day. They went the first day, but they didn't see the King. Second day—no King. Third day, fourth day, fifth day, sixth day…still no King. Finally, on the seventh day, they decided to go to the Secret Place instead of eating lunch. When they arrived, the door was open and the King was waiting for them...

"I had to make sure you *really* wanted this," he said, "because it is *not* going to be easy."

The King led Seeker and Moira to the window of the Secret Place and opened the golden shutters. To Seeker and Moira's surprise, although it was lunch-time, through that window they saw a beautiful night sky. Thousands of twinkling stars shone in the darkness. The King pointed, "Do you see those stars? I made them! And I call each one by name!"

Seeker and Moira looked up at the King with awe. "Wow!" they said together.

Then they looked again through the window of the Secret Place, and instead of the night sky, now they saw a stormy ocean. Lightning and thunder filled the scene, and powerful waves came crashing against the window of the Secret Place. Moira and Seeker hid behind the King so they wouldn't get wet.

The King lifted his hand and spoke to the storm, "Peace—be still," he said. And the winds and the waves went calm.

Seeker and Moira again looked up at the King with awe, "Wow!"

The next scene they saw through the window was a dark village. It seemed very sad and empty; and a lonely wind echoed through the streets. Seeker and Moira shivered. As they continued to peer through the dim light, they saw an old building that looked like a store. The sign above the front door was faded, and all of the windows were boarded shut.

They looked more closely, and were able to see inside the store. It was filled with piles of lumber and tools; and stacks of books and papers. Everything was covered in a blanket of dust and cobwebs. On a table in the middle of the room, the low flicker of a lantern was struggling to fight off the darkness.

And then, Seeker and Moira saw something else.

There, sitting on a chair, with chains around his body and his eyes half closed, was a man. His beard and hair had not been trimmed for a very long time, and at first Moira and Seeker didn't recognize him. Then Seeker gasped, "Dad! That's Dad!"

"Dad?" Moira echoed, "No, that can't be Dad; he doesn't have a beard…Wait a minute, Seeker, you're right. That is Dad! But he looks so awful!"

They watched Wanderer for a moment, shocked at his appearance. Then Seeker pointed and cried, "Look! Dragons!"

Two incredibly ugly dragons snarled as they came to stand by Wanderer. The dragons laughed viciously as they pulled the chains tighter, but Wanderer didn't seem to notice. He was almost asleep...

Seeker had learned about fighting dragons. When he saw those awful creatures beside his father, courage filled his heart! He would come against the dragons in the name of the King! Seeker began to roll up his sleeves when he felt a gentle hand on his shoulder. "No, Seeker," said the King. "Not this time. Your father *likes* those dragons."

"He *likes* those dragons?!" echoed Seeker and Moira together. "What?! How can he *like* them?!"

"Your father is living in a place called Despair. He never learned to overcome the obstacles; now the obstacles have overcome *him*...and he *likes* it that way. To him, it feels like he is in a safe place."

"He could get away if he wanted to," said Moira as she looked closer. "The chains aren't that tight. I guess maybe the dragons just make Dad *feel* like he can't move."

"How can they do that?" asked Seeker. "Why are those dragons so powerful, King? What are their names, anyway?"

"The dragons are Discouragement and Bitterness," the King explained. "When they first came to your father, they were quite small; but the more he listened to their voices, the stronger they became."

Seeker remembered the last dragon he had fought—the dragon Itsalmine. Seeker had saved up coins to buy something that he *really* wanted—a bow and arrow set. The dragon had tried to convince Seeker that the money was all his and that he deserved the best bow and arrow in the village; even though Doodle and Do desperately needed the same exact amount of money. Seeker shuddered, remembering. "King, if I would have kept listening to Itsalmine, would he have grown stronger?"

The King nodded. Seeker gulped and said, "What a scary thought. And by now I would have been...I would have been..."

"On your way to a very sad place, Seeker," said the King.

"Like Dad?" Moira asked.

"A similar place," the King nodded. "Your father lives in Despair...and he wants to stay that way. He has given up. Discouragement and Bitterness have overwhelmed him."

Moira looked up with tearful eyes. "But King! Can't you *make* him leave that place?!"

31

The King shook his head sadly, "No. Not until he really wants me to." Then the King wrapped his great arms around Seeker and Moira and began to sing...

Behold I hold the universe within my hands;

The mighty ocean waves are mine, I command them!

But when it comes to wandering hearts...

Those I will not claim

Until they really want me to...

I just stand...and wait.

Oh how I long for them to come to me;

Oh how I long for them to run to me!

Oh how I long for them to really see my Light-

But they are blinded...

Oh how I long for them to come to me;

Oh how I long for them to run to me!

Oh how I long for them to really see my Light.

As the King finished his song, Moira turned to him in desperation. "King, that's our father! We can't just leave him there! There must be something we can do! Isn't there something we can do, King?!"

The King looked at Seeker and Moira's earnest young faces, and nodded. "Yes. There is something you can do. I want you to continue to meet here every day in the Secret Place; and as you do, those dragons will not be able to lie to your father anymore. And, I want you to really believe that your father will read the Great Book. He used to read it. If he would just open it, I would speak to him."

"All right, King! We'll do it!"

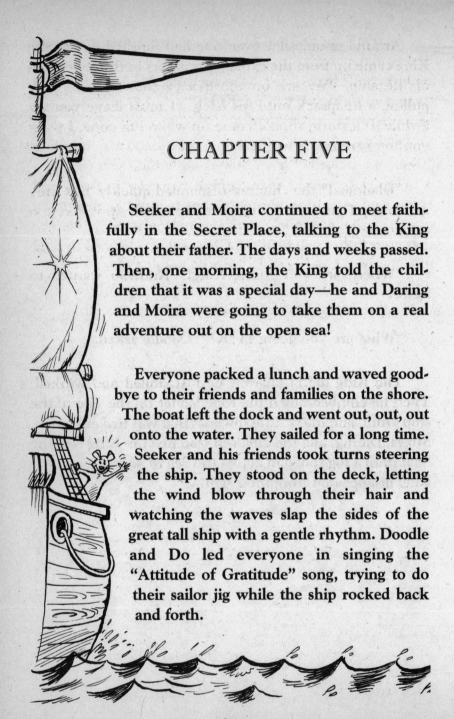

CHAPTER FIVE

Seeker and Moira continued to meet faithfully in the Secret Place, talking to the King about their father. The days and weeks passed. Then, one morning, the King told the children that it was a special day—he and Daring and Moira were going to take them on a real adventure out on the open sea!

Everyone packed a lunch and waved goodbye to their friends and families on the shore. The boat left the dock and went out, out, out onto the water. They sailed for a long time. Seeker and his friends took turns steering the ship. They stood on the deck, letting the wind blow through their hair and watching the waves slap the sides of the great tall ship with a gentle rhythm. Doodle and Do led everyone in singing the "Attitude of Gratitude" song, trying to do their sailor jig while the ship rocked back and forth.

Around noon, after everyone had finished lunch, the King came up from the captain's quarters in the lower part of the ship. "We are on the Sea of Sadness," he said, pulling a knapsack onto his back. "I must leave you for awhile. If a storm should come up while I'm gone, I want you to overcome it with…?"

"Gladness!" the children responded quickly. But they didn't slap Gladness on the back like usual; they were too curious.

"Where are you going, King?" KnowSo wanted to know.

"What are you going to DO?" Doodle asked.

The King didn't answer, he just smiled and winked. Then he climbed down the rope ladder on the side of the ship's hull, and into a little rowboat that was tied alongside. Moira, Daring, and the children watched the King row the boat until a fog rolled in across the Sea of Sadness, and the King disappeared from their sight.

CHAPTER SIX

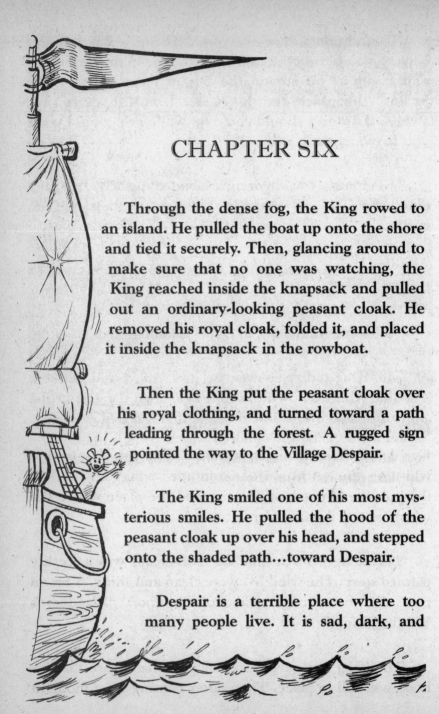

Through the dense fog, the King rowed to an island. He pulled the boat up onto the shore and tied it securely. Then, glancing around to make sure that no one was watching, the King reached inside the knapsack and pulled out an ordinary-looking peasant cloak. He removed his royal cloak, folded it, and placed it inside the knapsack in the rowboat.

Then the King put the peasant cloak over his royal clothing, and turned toward a path leading through the forest. A rugged sign pointed the way to the Village Despair.

The King smiled one of his most mysterious smiles. He pulled the hood of the peasant cloak up over his head, and stepped onto the shaded path...toward Despair.

Despair is a terrible place where too many people live. It is sad, dark, and

very lonely. But in that place, the King heard someone whistling the "Attitude of Gratitude" song! He walked through the streets until he reached the place where the whistling was coming from.

There, right in the middle of Despair, was a freshly painted store. The windows were clean and shiny. A brand new sign was hanging above the door: "Wanderer's Woodworking."

The King buttoned his cloak and made sure that his hood was still in place. Then, after pausing for a moment with another of his mysterious smiles, the King walked through the door…

The store looked much different than when Seeker and Moira had seen it through the window of the Secret Place. Everything was clean and tidy. The dust and cobwebs were gone; the tools were all neatly in their places; the books and papers were organized; and the Great Book was open on the table near the bright glow of the lantern.

In a far corner the dragons, Discouragement and Bitterness, were gagged and chained! The very chains they had used on Wanderer now covered them! When the dragons saw the King they squirmed in pain and cried, "Mmpphh!" The King smiled again.

Wanderer was bent over his workbench, busily making some bows and arrows. He looked up, saw the stranger in a cloak, and reached out his hand in greeting, "Good day, sir! My name is Wanderer. And you are….?"

"I am…*Answer!*" the King said, shaking Wanderer's hand firmly.

"Well, it's good to meet you, Answer! Is there anything I can help you with?"

The King picked up an arrow. "Tell me about what you have been working on today."

38

Wanderer proudly held up a bow and another arrow. "I make the best bows and arrows in the land, sir. Some of them are heavy and strong; others are lightweight, and all have great accuracy and balance. Each one is made for a special reason—a special purpose!"

"*Really?*" the King spoke thoughtfully, as he inspected the arrow. "You know, that reminds me of people. Every person is made for a special reason—a special purpose." Answer set the arrow down and turned toward Wanderer.

"What is *your* special purpose, Wanderer?"

Wanderer was surprised and suddenly felt very embarrassed. "Special purpose? Why...I don't know, sir! I suppose I have searched all my life for my special purpose; but I've never found it."

The King walked over to the Great Book, open on the table. The lantern beside it glowed even more brightly as the King approached. "Have you searched here, Wanderer?"

"I used to, sir," replied Wanderer, "and I have been again lately." Wanderer walked across the room and stood beside Answer and the Great Book. "You know, it tells the most amazing story about a King!"

"*Really?* Tell me about this King."

"Well, it seems that the King loved his people so much that he left his throne, left his Kingdom, and went right down to where they were!"

"Hmm..." said the King softly, "then what happened?"

"He made himself look like one of the people," Wanderer said, "He wore a disguise—so they didn't realize who he was..."

"I *see*," said the King.

Wanderer picked up the Great Book and continued, "The King did miracles, and told stories about his Kingdom. He explained to the people how much the King loved them—but they didn't understand..."

Wanderer shook his head sadly. "They didn't understand. I was just reading today, how the people turned against him. They took nails and put them into his hands and his feet and they...they killed him!" Wanderer set the Book back on the table, shaking his head in dismay. "They *killed* Him."

Slowly, the King pushed back the hood of his cloak and spoke softly, "He didn't stay dead, Wanderer."

Wanderer gasped, "Wh...what...?"

Then the King held out his hands—revealing two old and faded scars—and Wanderer whispered in amazement,

"King! You are the King...and not just the King; you are the *real* King...You are the King in the Great Book!"

The King nodded and spoke with gentle strength. "The King did not *stay* dead, Wanderer...and he is still the *Answer* to *everything* you have *ever* searched for."

Wanderer looked into the eyes of the King, took hold of the wounded hands, and knelt down. "Your Majesty," he said.

And as he knelt, the dragons in the corner grew smaller and smaller and smaller...until they disappeared.

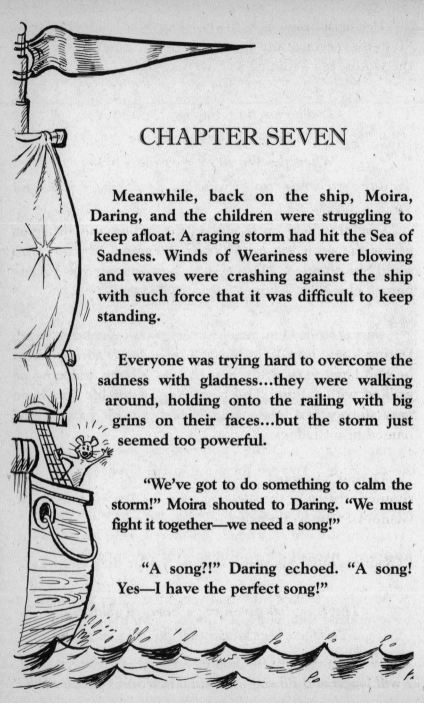

CHAPTER SEVEN

Meanwhile, back on the ship, Moira, Daring, and the children were struggling to keep afloat. A raging storm had hit the Sea of Sadness. Winds of Weariness were blowing and waves were crashing against the ship with such force that it was difficult to keep standing.

Everyone was trying hard to overcome the sadness with gladness...they were walking around, holding onto the railing with big grins on their faces...but the storm just seemed too powerful.

"We've got to do something to calm the storm!" Moira shouted to Daring. "We must fight it together—we need a song!"

"A song?!" Daring echoed. "A song! Yes—I have the perfect song!"

Daring shouted over the howling wind to the children, "Listen everyone, and join in singing! I don't know all of the words, but I think I know enough!"

I will overcome the Sea of Sadness;
Before it overcomes me
When the Winds of Weariness blow
And the waves rise up - I will sing, I will sing, I will sing!

Gladness held on tightly to the railing and struggled across the deck toward Moira and Daring. "I know this song!" he shouted. "This song is how my parents got my name! This song is how I became Gladness!"

Daring smiled and reached out to take the boy's hand. Daring knew how hard life had been for Gladness...how he had been very sick when he was a baby and now he walked with a limp. The beginning of his life had been very stormy, but in the middle of it all, his parents had named him Gladness.

Daring squeezed the boy's hand more tightly and shouted through the driving rain and wind. "Sing it, Gladness! Sing to the sadness!"

Gladness lifted his voice, singing louder than the wind.

The King has given me a heart of gladness
To face every storm that life may bring
I will dance and lift my hands; I will laugh and I'll sing!
I will laugh and I'll sing... I will laugh and I WILL SING!

43

44

As he sang, Gladness began to laugh. He laughed and he laughed and he laughed. He laughed so hard that everyone else just had to join in! Soon, they were having so much fun laughing and singing that it didn't matter how strong the storm was; it didn't matter how great the sadness was!

Then Seeker made a discovery—he found that they could actually sing to the waves! He leaned over the side of the ship, chose a wave and called straight toward it, "Sing!" and the wave went down!

"Hey, everyone!" he shouted. "You can sing to the waves! You can sing directly to the storm and your song is stronger than it is! Look!"

Seeker leaned over the railing of the ship, aimed, and shouted, "Sing!" The wave went calm. The others were impressed. Soon everyone was using their song to overcome the storm.

Seeker and Moira were standing together on the side of the ship, singing to the last few waves... "Sing!"..."Sing!" when Seeker looked off into the distance and suddenly cried, "Look! The King is coming back! The King is coming back!" Seeker looked more closely and caught his breath. "And....and...he's not...alone...!"

Seeker and Moira stood together with their hands clenched tightly and watched as the little rowboat got closer and closer. Daring and the children crowded around them, trying to see. "Who's with the King?" everyone wondered. The closer the rowboat came, the more tightly

Seeker and Moira clenched each other's hands. The person with the King was their father.

Everyone watched in silence as the rowboat came alongside *The Adventurer*. They watched as the King tied the boat securely to the ship and he and Wanderer climbed up the rope ladder. Then everyone stood back as Wanderer walked over to his children and stood silently in front of them. A moment of awkward silence passed, and then their father began to cry.

"Moira…Seeker. I'm so sorry," he said, "I am so *sorry*. I never learned to overcome the obstacles in my life. Instead, I let the obstacles overcome me. Please, will you forgive me?"

Moira and Seeker nodded through their tears and rushed to put their arms around him. "We forgive you, Dad! We forgive you."

Their father hugged Moira and Seeker close and said, "The King has come to me, and he's given me a new heart, and a new name! From now on, I am Steadfast!"

As Moira and Seeker stood in their father's arms, Daring and the children happily gathered around and joined in for a group hug. Then Steadfast reached into a satchel and pulled out a polished wooden bow and five arrows with tiny blue and red feathers on the ends. He turned to Seeker and said, "I wanted to give these to you, son. I've been working on this special set, and I was thinking about you the whole time while I worked. The King told me that you would REALLY like them."

"The King was right! Yes Dad, I REALLY like them! Thanks! Wow…these are nicer than any I've ever seen…"

Moira's eyes were shining. "Dad, it will be so good to have you back at home!"

"Well, Moira, the King and I talked about where I should live now. I'm back in the Kingdom, but I won't go home…not just yet…" Steadfast looked over at the King, who winked at him. "The King has given me a new name, but I need some time to grow into that name."

The King stepped forward. "Steadfast will stay in the castle with me for awhile, reading the Great Book and exploring. That way, he will grow stronger, and learn to overcome the obstacles he will face…"

"Before they overcome me!" Steadfast nodded. "I need to learn to be a good husband and a good father. I can't do it by myself."

Moira and Seeker were disappointed, but they understood. "Okay, Dad! We'll know right where to find you!"

"I'm sure GLAD Steadfast is in the Kingdom!" Gladness said.

"A feast has been prepared in the ship's dining hall to welcome Steadfast back to my Kingdom!" the King announced, taking Gladness by the hand. "Let's go and celebrate with Gladness! After all, it was Gladness who helped you all defeat the storm of Sadness!"

Gladness was amazed, "How did you know about that, King? You weren't even here during the storm!"

"*Really?*" asked the King, with his eyebrows raised and a smile playing at the corners of his mouth.

Everyone excitedly climbed down to the lower room of the ship. Sure enough, the ship's dining hall had been transformed into a huge banqueting hall. There was steaming hot food, minstrels, and lots of fun waiting for them.

Toward the end of the meal, while the minstrels played songs of the Kingdom, the King turned quietly to Seeker. He leaned forward, smiled one of his mysterious smiles, and winked, motioning for Seeker to follow him. Everyone was so busy talking and singing that they didn't notice the two of them slip up the stairs to the deck of the ship.

The sun was just starting to go down and the sky was full of beautiful colors. In the distance were the shores of the Kingdom. Seeker was sure that he could see his mother standing there, waving.

He waved back and turned excitedly to the King, "Wow! We sure have a surprise for her, don't we King!?"

"We sure do," agreed the King. "Oh, and Seeker, I want to give you something."

The King reached inside a pocket of his royal robe and pulled out...Seeker's model ship, perfectly mended and restored.

"Always remember, Seeker—I can put *anything* together that's been broken."

THINK ABOUT THE STORY

When bad things happen in our lives...in our families...the King wants to help us. He loves to fix things that are broken—especially broken hearts. Sometimes life can't be put back together like it used to be, but King Jesus certainly can put our hearts back together! He can make them even stronger than they were before the problem!

Despair is not a good place to live. If you ever find yourself there, get out! King Jesus is the Answer. Kneel before Him and any dragons—Discouragement, Bitterness, Fear, Anger, or Greed—will lose their power over you.

SEARCH THE PAGES OF THE GREAT BOOK (THE BIBLE)

Romans 12:21 - Don't let bad stuff overcome you!
John 14:6 - There is only one Answer!
Romans 12:12 - Don't give up!
Psalm 42 - Sing to your sadness!
(The Psalms are songs!)
Isaiah 61:1-2 - There is healing for broken hearts...

TALK TO THE KINGÖ

"Hi, King Jesus. Today I give you any broken pieces that are in my heart. I choose to trust You. I choose to sing to my sadness and I command the Winds of Weariness to stop blowing in my life. I refuse to live in Despair. I believe that You are the Way, the Truth and the Life. You are the Answer. Thank You, King Jesus. Thank You."

VERSES TO REMEMBER

(HUGGA-WUGGA ô PARAPHRASE)

*Be not overcome with evil; but
overcome evil with good!!
Romans 12:21 uh-huh, uh-huh;
Romans 12:21 uh-huh!*

*I speak to the sadness in my heart—
"Hey, HEART! You believe!"
I'll read some verses from Psalm 42 and
I-WILL-SING!*

Adventures in the Kingdom™
by Dian Layton

— SEEKER'S GREAT ADVENTURE
Seeker and his friends leave the CARNALville of Selfishness and begin the great adventure of really knowing the King!

— RESCUED FROM THE DRAGON
The King needs an army to conquer a very disgusting dragon and rescue the people who live in the Village of Greed.

— SECRET OF THE BLUE POUCH
The children of the Kingdom explore the pages of an ancient golden book and step through a most remarkable doorway — into a brand new kind of adventure!

— IN SEARCH OF WANDERER
Come aboard the sailing ship *The Adventurer*, and find out how Seeker learns to fight dragons through the window of the Secret Place.

— THE DREAMER
Moira, Seeker's older sister, leaves the Kingdom and disappears into the Valley of Lost Dreams. Can Seeker rescue his sister before it's too late?

— ARMOR OF LIGHT
In the World Beyond the Kingdom, Seeker must use the King's weapons to fight the dragons Bitterness and Anger to save the life of one young boy.

— CARRIERS OF THE KINGDOM
Seeker and his friends discover that the Kingdom is within them! In the Land of Laws Forgotten they meet with Opposition, and the children battle against some very nasty dragons who do not want the people to remember...

Available at your local Christian bookstore.

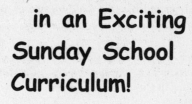

55

The Young God Chasers
Curriculum Series by Dian Layton

Seeking the King

(With quotes and concepts from *The God Chasers* by Tommy Tenney) Many children who attend church "live in the Kingdom, but don't know the King." A God Chaser is a "SEEKER"! The lessons in this first binder are designed to encourage hunger in the children's hearts to really KNOW (not just know ABOUT) King Jesus!

The King and His Kingdom

(With quotes and concepts from *The God Chasers* by Tommy Tenney) Children need to hear what is on the King's heart and then DO what He tells them to do...not just "some day when they grow up"; but NOW! Children can be part of His "very big little army" and have a powerful impact on the world around them!

Seeker's Sources of Power

(With quotes and concepts from *Secret Sources of Power* by Tommy Tenney) The concept of having POWER is intriguing to children. How valuable for youngsters to learn that the true source of power is being emptied of self and filled up with Jesus! They will learn how to live a POWER-FILLED life every day!

Seeker's Secret Place

(With quotes and concepts from *Secret Sources of Power* by Tommy Tenney) Many people spend time in counseling sessions trying to get free of the guilt, worry, fear, and sin they have been carrying around for years. In this curriculum, children learn how to "cast all their cares" and "unload their heavy burdens" on Jesus.

Watch for these titles at your local Christian bookstore.

For more information and sample chapters, visit www.destinyimage.com or www.seeker.org

56